KU-252-020

Little Blue

and the Terrible Jokes

Written by

Margaret Ryan

Illustrated by

Andy Ellis

*Hodder
Children's
Books*

A division of Hodder Headline Limited

For Colin
with love
M.R.

For Freddie
A.E.

ABERDEENSHIRE LIBRARY & INFORMATION SERVICE	
12 05341	
CBS	20/08/2002
Junior Star	4.99
JSP	OLDP

Little Blue was reading his comic
one morning when…

TAP TAP TAP

…there was a knock on the door

of the upturned boat where

he lived.

Little Blue opened the door and
looked out.

"That's funny," he said,
"there's nobody there. I was sure
I heard someone knocking."

He closed the door and went
back to his comic.

He was just reading all about the
adventures of Super Blue Penguin
when...

TAP TAP TAP

...there was another knock
at the door.

Little Blue opened the door and
looked out.

"That's funny," he said, "there's
still nobody there. I was sure
I heard someone knocking."

He closed the door and went
back to his comic.

He was just reading all about
Super Blue Penguin escaping
from the sharks when...

TAP TAP TAP

...there was a third knock
at the door.

Little Blue opened the door, and
S P L O O S H a bucketful
of water hit him in the face.

"Cousin Penni," spluttered
Little Blue. "I should have known
it was you!"

"I knocked on your door with
a long stick while I hid round
the corner," giggled Penni.
"That was funny!"
"No it wasn't," said Little Blue.

But Penni wasn't listening.
"Come on, Little Blue,"
she said. "Let's hop down to
the shore."
They had only hopped a little
way when...

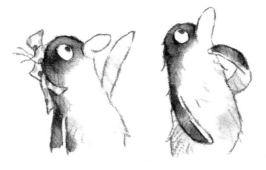

"Look, Little Blue" said Penni.
"What's that up in the sky?"
"What? Where?" Little Blue
looked up. "I don't see any..."

Penni stuck out a foot and
tripped up Little Blue.

"Ha ha ha, enjoy your trip,"
giggled Penni. "That was funny!"

Little Blue got up and rubbed
his beak.

"No it wasn't," he muttered.

But Penni wasn't listening.

Little Blue and Penni found
Rocky, the rockhopper penguin,
having a quiet snooze on the
rocks by the water's edge.

"Wakey wakey, sleepyhead,"
yelled Penni in his ear.

"What's up, what's the matter...?
Oh, Penni," said Rocky. "I should
have known it was you. I was
having a nice sleep, too."

"Never mind that," said Penni.

"I know a penguin joke. Want to hear it?"

"No," said Rocky and Little Blue.

But Penni wasn't listening.

"WHAT'S BLACK AND WHITE
AND BLACK AND WHITE?"

"Don't know," muttered Rocky
and Little Blue.

"A PENGUIN ROLLING DOWN
A HILL!" Penni giggled.

"Here's another one.

WHAT'S BLACK AND WHITE
AND LAUGHING?"

"Don't know," muttered Rocky
and Little Blue again.

"ANOTHER PENGUIN WHO
PUSHED THE FIRST ONE,"
giggled Penni, and she pushed
Little Blue off the rocks so that
he rolled down into the sea.

"Ha ha ha. That was funny!"
giggled Penni.

"No it wasn't," muttered
Little Blue.

But Penni wasn't listening.

"Come on," she said. "I'm starving.

Let's go fishing. I bet I can catch

more fish than you, Little Blue."

"Bet you can't!" said Little Blue.

The three penguins dived into

the water and all came up with

a mouthful of fish.

"I caught one," said Rocky.

"I caught two," said Little Blue.

"I caught THREE," said Penni,
but swallowed them quickly
before Little Blue could count.

Just then two dark triangular
shapes appeared in the water.
"Oh no," said Little Blue.
"It's the sharks, Fick and Fin.
And I think they've spotted us!"

They had.
They swam a little closer.
"Do you see what I see, Fick?"
said Fin.

"I see the sea, Fin," said Fick.

"Apart from that," said Fin.

"Let me see," said Fick. "Oh,
I know. I see one, two, four
penguins."

"You're not very good
at counting, are you, Fick?"
said Fin. "There are only three
penguins."

"That's still one each for lunch,
Fin," said Fick.

"Let's get them!" said Fin, and
they swam swiftly towards the

three penguins,

teeth bared

and ready.

"SHARK ATTACK SHARK
ATTACK!" yelled Little Blue.
"Quick, dive down through
the seaweed tunnels. It's too
narrow in there for the sharks
to follow."
The three penguins dived down
and swam through the seaweed
tunnels. Just in time!

It was scary in there. Big eyes
blinked at them from black holes.
Big claws nipped at them from
black rocks.

And there was LOTS of
seaweed. Slippy seaweed,
sloppy seaweed, slimy seaweed.
It hung from the roof. It clung
to the walls. It curled itself round
and round the penguins as they
swam past.

But eventually they popped
up, covered in seaweed,
on the other side.

"I don't like the seaweed
tunnels," said Rocky.
"They're scary," said Little Blue.
"Huh, you're just a scaredy cat,
Little Blue," smirked Penni.
"I thought they were fun!"

25

"Now what shall we do?"
said Penni, as they waddled up
the beach. "I'm bored."
"We could go to the parkland
and visit Joey," said
Little Blue.

"I know a
good joke about a kangaroo,"
said Penni. "Want to hear it?"
"No," said Rocky and
Little Blue.
But Penni wasn't listening.

"WHAT DO YOU GIVE A KANGAROO WITH BIG FEET?"

"Don't know," muttered Rocky and Little Blue.

"PLENTY OF ROOM!"

"Ha ha ha. That was funny!" giggled Penni.

"No it wasn't," said Rocky and Little Blue.

Joey, the little kangaroo, had his head and one foot sticking out of his mother's pouch when the three penguins arrived.

"Hi," said Joey. "The rest of me will be out in a minute. I'm just looking for my other leg. It's in here somewhere. Ah, found it."

And he hopped out of the pouch.

Then he started to scratch.

"I think I've got a flea," he said.

"I know a joke about a flea,"
said Penni. "Want to hear it?"

"No," said Joey, Rocky and
Little Blue.

But Penni wasn't listening.

"HOW DO YOU START
A FLEA RACE?"

"Don't know," muttered Joey,
Rocky and Little Blue.

"ONE, TWO, FLEA, GO!"

"Ha ha ha. That was funny!" said
Penni. "NOW what shall we do?"

"We could play hide-and-seek,"
said Rocky and Joey. "We like
that."

"Or we could play chase,"
said Little Blue. "I like that."

"That's a baby's game, Little
Blue," said Penni. "I could tell
you more jokes."

But before they could decide
there was a noise like distant
thunder.

"Oh no," said Joey. "It's Big Grey
and his mob! Quick, jump into
the swamp before those big
kangaroos knock us over."

"Jump into the swamp?" said
Penni. "I'm not jumping into
the swamp. It's too smelly."
"And now it's too late," said
Little Blue. "They've seen us."
Big Grey and his mob thundered
up and surrounded them.

"What have we here?" said
Big Grey.
"Looks like three penguins and
a little Joey," said his mob.
"I can see that," said Big Grey.
"And what are you four doing?"

"Nothing," said Joey.

"Nothing at all," said Rocky.

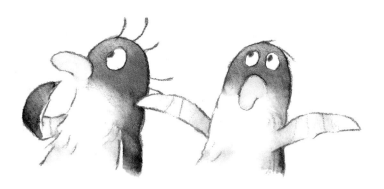

"Absolutely nothing at all,"
said Little Blue.

"Actually I was just going
to tell them a kangaroo joke,"
said Penni. "Want to hear it,
Big Grey?"
"Oh no," said Little Blue.
But Penni wasn't listening.

"WHAT DO YOU CALL A BIG GREY KANGAROO WITH FOUR NOSES, FIVE MOUTHS AND SIX EARS?"

"I don't know," said Big Grey. "What DO you call a big grey kangaroo with four noses, five mouths and six ears?"

"UGLY," giggled Penni. "Ha ha
ha. That was really funny!"

"Oh no it wasn't," said
Little Blue.

"Now I've got a joke for YOU,"
said Big Grey.
"WHAT IS BIG AND GREY
AND LAUGHING?"

"Don't know," said Penni.

"A BIG GREY KANGAROO
THROWING A PENGUIN
INTO THE SEA!"

And he picked up Penni,
carried her down to the sea
and threw her in.

Rocky and Joey and Little Blue
hurried down to the sea after her.

Penni bobbed up, coughing and
spluttering and covered in smelly
seaweed. The three friends looked
at her and started to laugh.

"That wasn't funny," muttered
Penni.

"Oh yes it was," giggled
Little Blue. "Ha ha ha."